From Cow to Cone
SOLVING THE MILK MYSTERY

WRITTEN AND ILLUSTRATED BY
STACIE DESAUTELS

FROM COW TO CONE
Solving the Milk Mystery

Copyright © 2015 Vanderwende Farms
Written and illustrated by Stacie Desautels

ISBN 978-1-886068-99-5 (soft cover)
ISBN 978-1-886068-98-8 (hardback)
Library of Congress Control Number: 2015953513

Edited by Candy Abbott and Pam Halter

Fruitbearer Kids, a Division of
Fruitbearer Publishing, LLC
P.O. Box 777, Georgetown, DE 19947
302.856.6649 • FAX 302.856.7742
www.fruitbearer.com • info@fruitbearer.com

Printed in the United States of America

Dedicated to

WILLIAM AND ELLEN VANDERWENDE
WHO STARTED THE FARM IN 1954
WITH SIX COWS AND $35.

It was a magical, moonlit night in Bridgeville, Delaware. Stars twinkled, crickets chirped, and frogs sang. Most of the world was asleep . . . but not the cows on the Vanderwende Farm. They were wide awake and pacing.

5

"Come on girls, it's midnight. Let's get a move on."

Farmer Jimmy always sounded cheerful, even in the wee hours.

6

Queenie mooed. "Here we go again."

"I know, here we go *again*." Shamrock
yawned.

Daisy lifted her legs extra high and pretended to march.

"We're a cow parade!"

A Cow Parade!

Lovey giggLed.

"Mooooove out!"

Farmer Jimmy guided the girls into the milking barn.

"Let's get you hooked up, milked, and back to bed."

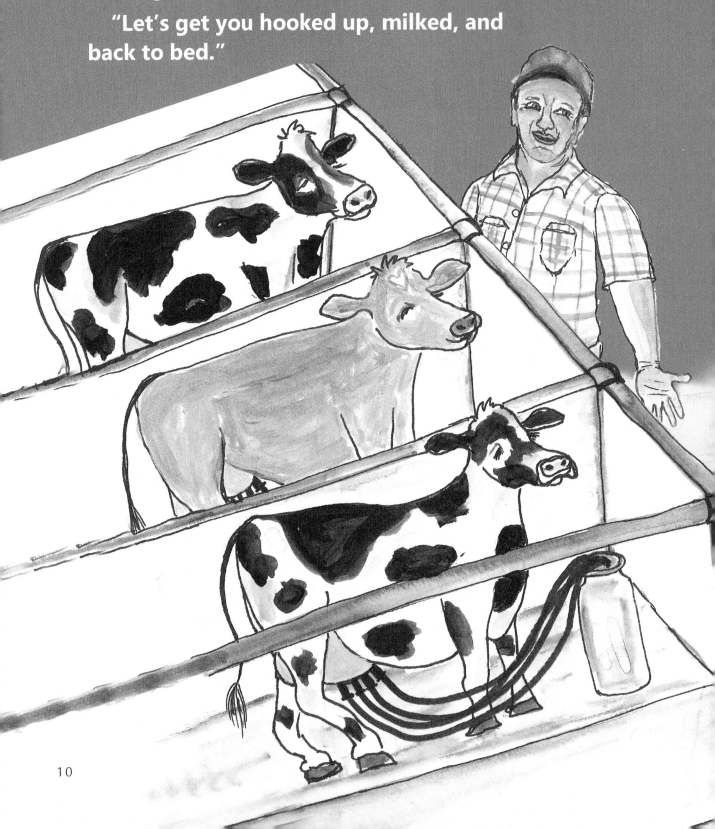

"*AHHHHH*, that feels so much better." Daisy mooed as the milk flowed into the tank.

Queenie swished her tail. "Carrying all this milk around is hard. I'm glad to get rid of it."

11

As soon as the cows were unhooked, Jesse, the eldest Vanderwende son, guided them back to the field.

"Okay, girls, back we go. Time to get a few more winks of sleep."

"Mmmmooooooo. Sweet dreams girlfriends," Lovey said with a yawn.

The sun was just peeking over the field when the herd awoke to a most irritating sound.

"Chirp, chirp, chirp . . . tweet, tweet, tweet. Good morning, good morning, good morning!"

Shamrock opened one eye. "Go away!"

"Wendell, you know we don't get up this early." Queenie swatted her tail at the bird.

"This is a brand new day! Be glad and rejoice! Get up!" Wendell chirped right in Queenie's ear.

"Mmmooooooo. I will rejoice after I get some peace and quiet," she said.

Wendell swooped low, looking eye-to-eye with Queenie. "All creatures should be up by now!"

"Okay, okay." Queenie blinked. "I will get up. But only because I'm hungry. What do you want, you annoying little bird?"

Wendell hopped down to the fence in the pasture as the cows gathered around. He puffed out his chest.

"Did I hear one of you say you wondered what the farmer does with the milk he collects from you every day, twice a day?"

Queenie mooed. "You busy-body. I only mumbled that to myself."

"You know, I have wondered about that, too,"
Daisy said, blinking her big brown eyes.

"It's quite a mystery," Shamrock said.

Wendell fluffed his feathers.
"I have a great idea.
You know what? I can fly!"

Queenie couldn't help rolling her eyes. "Imagine that, Wendell. Birds can fly."

20

Wendell gave a short laugh. "You know I can fly, but did you know I can . . . *spy?*"

"What do you mean, dear?" Lovey asked.

Wendell ruffled his feathers. "What if I followed the workers to see where they take all your milk and find out what they do with it?"

The cows mooed with excitement.

Shamrock frowned. "What if we don't like what they do with our milk?"

"What can we do about it?" Queenie said.
Then she turned to Wendell.
"Go ahead, if you are so smart. Fly and spy."

"Well, I could . . . but, what's in it for me?"

"If you could solve this mystery, we would be your friends," Lovey said sweetly.

"Be his friends?" Queenie moooed long and low. "Speak for yourself, Lovey."

Just then, Cody, the middle Vanderwende son, came up behind them. "Come on, Queenie, it's time to round up the girls and head to the barn for your noon milking."

Wendell hovered in front of Queenie's face as she moved forward.

She glared back. "Wendell, seriously. What will it take for you to solve the mystery of our milk?"

Wendell gave her a lopsided grin. "I want a best friend, and I want it to be *you*."

"Best friend? Don't push it, Wendell. You should be happy to be my friend."

"That's good enough for me," Wendell said as he swooped high and flew loop-dee-loop above the herd.

Queenie scowled and switched her tail all the way to the barn while the other cows danced in anticipation. But Lovey smiled and said softly, "Wendell will solve the milk mystery!"

As the cows were milked, Wendell hovered overhead. He flew near the milking machine and watched the milk go through a tube into a cooling tank that was put on a truck.

Then the truck began to move!

"Here I go!"
Wendell sped above the truck.

"I am so excited. I can't wait to solve the Milk Mystery!"

The truck pulled up to a huge building with a big sign that read, *Pasteurizing Plant.* Wendell didn't know what that meant, so he flew around the building looking for a way to get inside.

Wendell entered a super clean area and watched the milk go into huge metal drums and flow through pipes.

He flew a little farther and saw the milk, now steamy hot, go through a tube into a cooling tank and then into hundreds of milk jugs on a moving conveyor belt.

Outside, Wendell followed the milk jugs, which were placed in refrigerated trucks. Workers talked about delivering the jugs to different places so the milk could be made into butter, cheese, yogurt, and ice cream.

One of the drivers said, "This pasteurized milk goes to the Vanderwende Farm Creamery."

Oh!" Wendell said. "That's my farm!"

Wendell took a short cut and flew as fast as he could to the Vanderwende Farm. By the time he got there, the man was unloading the milk jugs.

Farmer Jimmy's wife came outside and the milk man said, "Hi Donna, I have your delivery."

"Thank you," she said. "The milk goes in the walk-in refrigerator."

Wendell waited until the milk man left and then flew through the back door just before it closed. He heard Donna say from the other room, "Taylor and Morgan, we're running low on vanilla ice cream."

What is ice cream? Wendell wondered.

"WHat iS ice CReaM?"

Taylor came out with a jug of milk, sugar, and strawberries. She loaded the ingredients into the machine, and they swirled around and around and around.

Morgan said, "We're low on Peanut Butter Fudge Ripple, too," as she gathered peanut butter, sugar, chocolate, and more milk.

Will, the youngest son, pulled the vanilla ice cream out of the walk-in freezer.

Wendell watched as Taylor put some ice cream in a bowl. When she said, "I need a spoon," and stepped away, he flew over to inspect the pink stuff. He leaned down . . . closer . . . and closer . . . and stuck his beak right into the ice cream.

"Brrrr, that is COLD!" he cried. "But, oh, goodness! It is so YUMMY!"

"Soooo Yummy!"

Taylor came back, tasted the ice cream, and smiled. She even kept smiling after she spotted Wendell.

"Out with you—no birds allowed!" she said and shooed him out of the creamery work station.

But Wendell didn't leave. He hid on a high shelf in the Ice Cream Parlor where he had the perfect bird's eye view. So many people. All eating different colors of ice cream!

A young man licked brown ice cream that sat on top of a pointy thing called a cone. "This is the best chocolate ice cream I have ever tasted," he said.

His girlfriend took a bite of her sundae. "Look how much they gave us. *It doesn't get any better than this!*"

A little girl sat daintily at a table for three with her parents. "Mommy, I love my pink strawberry sundae."

Another girl stood in front of a glass window. "I'll have a Raspberry Rumble in a homemade waffle cone."

"Coming right up," Donna said with a smile.

Wendell flew as fast as he could to the pasture.

"Wake up! Wake up! Wake up!
I solved the milk mystery!"

The cows hung on every word as Wendell shared how he flew above the milk truck and spied on what happened at the pasteurizing plant.

"Some milk goes to the store for people to drink, and some is made into food they eat—like cheese and butter and yogurt. But, the best part is what your milk is made into right here at Vanderwende Farms . . .

Ice Cream!"

He could scarcely catch his breath as he told the cows how good the ice cream tasted, the beautiful colors, the tasty flavors, the variety of toppings, and how much the people love it!

"How udderly wonderful!" Daisy said.

Lovey batted her long eyelashes. "No wonder they need so much milk from us every day, twice a day."

Shamrock winked at Wendell. "Makes me tired just thinking about it. But you're one brave bird, and I'm honored to call you my friend."

All the cows cheered.

"The milk mystery is solved!"

"Wendell is the greatest!"

Queenie's voice went soft.

"Wendell," she said, "this is truly amazing. If not for you, we would never have known how much our milk is appreciated. Will you forgive me for being unkind to you?"

"Are you serious? Oh, my goodness!" Wendell flapped and flew in circles. "Can you believe it? Queenie wants me to be her best friend!"

"Wendell, don't push it," Queenie gave him a lopsided smile. "I never agreed to be your *best* friend."

Wendell's smile broadened. "I know you don't mean it," he said as he shot into the air.

Queenie went on. "If you could manage to get us a sample of ice cream, I'll think about it."

The cows burst into laughter.

Wendell gazed at Queenie over his wing. "What flavor would you like?"

The End

*Mooo*velous Facts About Cows

- Holsteins are black and white or red and white; each has a unique pattern. No two are exactly the same.
- A Holstein calf weighs 80-110 lbs. at birth.
- A mature Holstein cow weighs 1,300-1,500 lbs.
- The Vanderwende farm has about 225 registered Holstein cows.

- Jerseys cows are a light to dark brown and often splashed with white. They look a little like a deer.
- Young cows are generally known as calves. Adult females are generally called cows.
- A cow must have a calf in order to produce milk. Calves are fed milk until they are 8-9 weeks old.
- The best cows give over 25 gallons of milk each day. That's 400 glasses of milk!
- The average cow is 2 years old when she has her first calf. A young female cow is called a heifer.
- Before milking machines were invented in 1894, farmers could only milk about 6 cows per hour. Today, farmers use machines to milk more than 100 cows per hour.
- A Jersey calf weighs around 60 pounds at birth.
- A mature Jersey cow weighs 900-1,000 pounds.
- The Vanderwende farm has about 30 Jersey cows.
- Cattle (cows) are herbivores that eat vegetation such as grass and grains.
- Cow stomachs have four chambers which help break down what they eat.
- There over 1 billion cattle in the world.
- Cows are sacred in India.
- In Ireland, there are about 2 cows for every person.
- Adult males that are not castrated are generally called bulls.
- Cows are milked for an average of 3-4 years.
- Cows drink about a bathtub full of water and eat around 40 pounds of food a day.

CrossWord Puzzle

ACROSS

1. White creamy drink from the cow udder?
3. How many times a day are the cows milked?
5. Colorful confetti topping for ice cream?
7. Ice cream flavor?
11. Dairy food usually served with fruit?
13. What type of cow has random spots is usually black and white or red and white?
15. Dairy food usually put on a sandwich.

DOWN

2. A cold creamy treat?
4. Black and white Holstein with a flower spot?
6. Sweet Jersey cow with a heart on her head?
8. Who solved the milk mystery?
9. Dairy product you put on toast?
10. Bossy cow in the book?
12. Red Holstein cow with an Irish clover spot?
14. What type of cow is a light brown and looks like a deer?

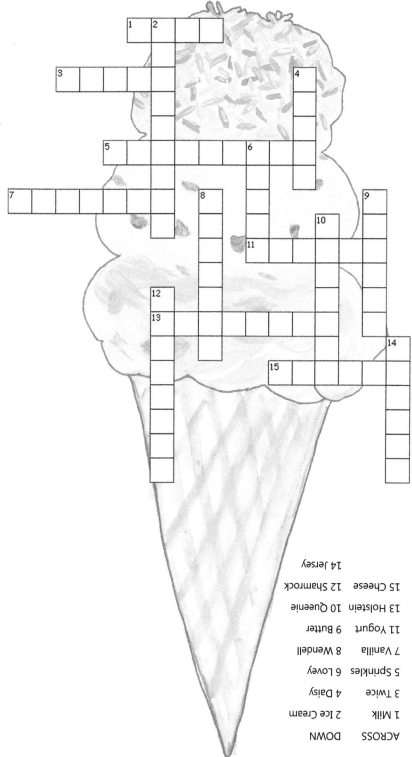

ACROSS	DOWN
1 Milk	2 Ice Cream
3 Twice	4 Daisy
5 Sprinkles	6 Lovey
7 Vanilla	8 Wendell
11 Yogurt	9 Butter
13 Holstein	10 Queenie
15 Cheese	12 Shamrock
	14 Jersey

Word Search

```
T  M  U  S  N  S  Q  E  R  V  E  W  Y  N  C
R  T  A  R  H  U  T  O  S  D  V  R  M  I  H
U  S  A  E  E  A  C  R  N  E  E  G  R  E  O
G  B  U  E  R  K  M  E  A  M  E  E  A  T  C
O  C  N  N  Y  C  W  R  A  W  T  H  F  S  O
Y  I  O  R  D  R  E  E  O  T  B  I  C  L  L
E  M  O  N  E  A  R  C  U  C  Q  E  E  O  A
Q  A  L  D  E  C  E  B  I  X  K  F  R  H  T
D  V  N  B  R  O  W  N  S  W  I  S  S  R  E
Z  A  H  O  T  F  U  D  G  E  D  A  I  S  Y
V  N  J  E  R  S  E  Y  L  L  E  D  N  E  W
K  I  I  T  Y  N  F  D  B  H  S  S  A  R  G
X  L  X  A  S  E  L  K  N  I  R  P  S  M  C
O  L  I  M  R  H  M  H  E  Y  E  V  O  L  O
P  A  J  M  M  G  H  E  R  D  R  I  T  U  W
```

BARN
BROWNSWISS
BUTTER
CHEESE
CHOCOLATE
CONE
COW
CREAMERY
DAISY
FARM
FIELD
GRAIN
GRASS
HERD
HOLSTEIN
HOTFUDGE
ICECREAM
JERSEY
LOVEY
MILK
QUEENIE
ROCKYROAD
SHAMROCK
SPRINKLES
STRAWBERRY
SUNDAE
VANDERWENDE
VANILLA
WENDELL
YOGURT

Meet the
AutHor/ILLuStrator
Stacie Desautels

A **Personal Note from Stacie:** I fell in love with the Vanderwende Family Farm the first time I visited. It was so charming, just like a fairy tale. I knew immediately that I wanted it to be my next book. As the manuscript came to life, I created each character with traits and symbolic references that would be fun for the reader: Wendell's name came from the Vander**wende** family name. Queenie's personality as the bossy Holstein, reflects her role as the "queen bee" of the herd. Lovey is the sweet Jersey cow with a heart on her forehead. Daisy, the ditzy holstein, is fashioned after my dog that looks like a cow. Shamrock, the red holstein, reflects Irish traits with a shamrock on her chest. While every cow is different, I used these symbols to identify each one because Farmer Jimmy told me that they all have unique personalities. Everyone seems to share my fondness for the Vanderwendes and their ice cream.

Daisy DeZigns Art Studio

Stacie is the colorful, whimsical artist of Daisy DeZigns Art Studio in Salisbury, Maryland. Her style is fresh, magical, and full of swirling colors designed to delight the viewer. She has illustrated the unique images for the Autumn Wine Festival posters and t-shirts at Pemberton Park for 12 years. Stacie has also illustrated four children's books: *Blue Bear Finds a Rainbow* and *Pink Bear's Journey* by McKenzie Betts, *Dayspring: Fearfully & Wonderfully Made* by Indya Rennie, and *The Christmas Hippo* by Lisa Williams.

One of Stacie's favorite items is her inspirational line of thought for the day cards called "Mindful Moments" which comes with a desktop easel to display your card of choice. Desautels has painted murals for Oak Ridge Baptist Church's children's areas and the HALO Shelter. During the week Stacie is the event planner for the Wicomico Civic Center focusing on meetings, weddings, parties and church events. For custom projects or to purchase any of her products please give Stacie a call at 443.783.9518 or email staciedesautels@aol.com.

Vanderwende Farm Creamery

www.vanderwendefarmcreamery.com

302.349.5110

Now with three locations:

- 4003 Seashore Highway, Bridgeville, Delaware
- 23 Bellevue Street, Dewey Beach, Delaware
- 8374 Hickman Road, Greenwood, DE 19550 *(coming in 2016)*

Vanderwendes History

We are a family-owned and operated, three-generation business, with the help of some other very dedicated employees. William and Ellen Vanderwende purchased this farm in 1954, starting with six cows and $35. The farm has since grown to about 4,000 acres and 225 registered Holstein cows which we milk twice a day. Our family has not only taken great pride in producing great quality milk, but we also take pride in being good stewards to the land. Among our many environmental practices are cover crop and nutrient management programs. We then decided to take our LOVE for both farming and the land and venture into another business:

Ice Cream!

CPSIA information can be obtained at www.ICGtesting.com
Printed in the USA
BVOW11s1434221015

423715BV00002B/2/P